x   Herman, Charlotte
        Millie Cooper, take a chance.

Millie Cooper,
TAKE A CHANCE

OTHER BOOKS BY CHARLOTTE HERMAN

Millie Cooper, TAKE A CHANCE

by Charlotte Herman

illustrated by Helen Cogancherry

E. P. DUTTON   NEW YORK

The editor and publisher have made every effort to trace ownership of "Hide and Seek" by Robin Christopher, a portion of which appears on page 93. The poem was originally published by Jarrolds.

Text copyright © 1988 by Charlotte Herman
Illustrations copyright © 1988 by Helen Cogancherry

Library of Congress Cataloging-in-Publication Data

Herman, Charlotte.
    Millie Cooper, take a chance / by Charlotte Herman; illustrated by Helen Cogancherry.—1st ed.
        p. cm.
    Summary: In 1947, after trying two different ways to win a bicycle and forcing herself to read a poem in front of her third grade class, Millie recognizes the importance of taking chances to make her life more interesting and satisfying.
    ISBN 0-525-44442-4
    [1. Assertiveness (Psychology)—Fiction. 2. Self-confidence—Fiction. 3. Apartment houses—Fiction. 4. Chicago (Ill.)—Fiction.] I. Cogancherry, Helen, ill. II. Title.
PZ7.H4313Mk 1988   88-11081
[Fic]—dc19   CIP
                                                          AC

Published in the United States by
E. P. Dutton, New York, N.Y.,
a division of NAL Penguin Inc.

Published simultaneously in Canada by
Fitzhenry & Whiteside Limited, Toronto

Printed in the U.S.A.   First Edition
10 9 8 7 6 5 4 3 2 1

to the newlyweds,
Sharon and Harvey
and for
Michael, Debbie, and Karen

Contents

The Bicycle Contest

Millie Cooper put on her Mickey Mouse ear-muffs and went out into the cold. She scooped up a handful of snow and smoothed it round to make a perfect snowball. She aimed it at a tree and missed. She was working on her second perfect snowball when her mother came out, wearing her skunk coat. They were going to walk over to Roosevelt Road to buy Millie a snow shovel at Woolworth's. Millie loved to play with sand shovels in the summer and snow shovels in the winter. She had recently broken her last shovel when she used it to slide down the hill on Douglas Boulevard.

"You won't have much of a season left," said Mrs. Cooper as they were walking. "Spring will be here next month."

Millie smiled up at her mother. "Does spring mean I can get my two-wheeler?" She gave a little skip. Last year she had begged her mother and father for a two-wheel bicycle, and they had told her to "wait until next year." Well, now it was next year—1947. And bicycles were on Millie's mind.

"Maybe for your birthday," said Mrs. Cooper.

"My birthday isn't until June. Think of all the good riding days I'll miss in March, April, and May. Maybe you can get me my present a few months early."

"Maybe . . . I don't know. Those two-wheel bicycles make me nervous. I worry that you'll fall off and get hurt. And I worry about cars." Her mother was stalling again. Just like she had last year.

"I'm not dumb enough to ride on the boulevard," Millie assured her. "I'll just ride on the sidewalk, or on Thirteenth Street, where there are hardly any cars. And I'll ride with both hands on the handlebars." It was the same argument she had used over and over again.

When they reached Woolworth's, Millie headed right for the shovels. She knew just where they were. She picked out a shovel exactly like the one she had broken. It was small, just the right size for her, and on the front was a picture of a winter scene, with a snowman sporting a high hat, a scarf, and a carrot nose. Millie took the shovel over to the cash register, where her mother was waiting.

"Shall I wrap it up or do you want to take it as is?" the saleslady asked.

Millie always liked to use her purchases right away. But she knew that her mother usually had her things wrapped or put into bags. Maybe that was the grown-up thing to do. She didn't want the saleslady to think she was a baby, who was so excited about buying a shovel that she couldn't wait to use it. She could act as grown-up as anyone.

"Wrap it, please," she said.

The saleslady put the shovel into a paper bag and tied it with a string. The long red handle stuck out, and Millie took hold of it.

As soon as she was out the door, Millie ripped off the bag and dumped it into a trash basket. Then, with the shovel in front of her, she began clearing a path toward home.

"If you were going to use the shovel right away, why did you make the clerk wrap it up?" her mother asked.

"I wasn't sure I'd be using it until now," answered Millie. She didn't want her mother to think she was a baby, either. A baby wouldn't be able to get a two-wheeler.

A few snowflakes began to fall, and Millie made sure to keep well away from her mother's coat. She was convinced that it smelled just like a skunk whenever it got wet—sort of like the smell in the Small Mammal House at the Brookfield Zoo.

It was dark by the time they got home. Millie stood her shovel in the kitchen next to the door. Then she took her coat off, went into the dining room, and turned on the radio. She kept her Mickey Mouse earmuffs on. They made her ears feel cozy.

Millie loved listening to all her favorite programs: "Jack Armstrong," "The Lone Ranger," "Captain Midnight." But lately she especially looked forward to hearing a certain announcement. There was a contest being held called Name Your Bicycle. Whoever came up with the best name for a bicycle won a brand-new two-wheeler. Actually, two bicycles were going to be given away, one to a boy and one to a girl. This was the last week of the contest, and so far Millie hadn't come up with a name she thought sounded like a winner.

While Millie was listening to a Wheaties commercial, her mother came into the dining room and handed her a tangerine. Millie enjoyed listening to the radio and eating tangerines at the same time.

"Don't you think you'd be able to hear the radio better if you took your earmuffs off?" her mother asked.

"I can hear perfect with them on," said Millie as she began peeling. She popped a section of the tangerine into her mouth.

By the time she was finished with the tangerine, the contest announcement came on. "Don't forget, boys and girls," the announcer said, "you may enter as many times as you like. But each entry must be on a separate postcard or in a separate envelope. All cards and envelopes must be postmarked by midnight, Saturday, February fifteenth. That's just a little over a week away, boys and girls, so hurry up with those entries."

Millie turned off the radio and went into the kitchen. She sat down on the window seat that overlooked the courtyard of her apartment building. The window seat was Millie's favorite thinking place. She opened her notebook and studied the list of bicycle names she had thought of so far. The three best were:

Rocket   (named after her Reynolds Rocket ballpoint pen, which she loved even though it didn't work)

Spitfire (a famous airplane used in the Second World War, which had ended just two years ago)

Atom   (a word everyone seemed to be using lately)

Millie liked these names, but she thought they were the kinds of names other people might send in. She needed something more unusual.

"Mama, what could I name my bicycle?"

Mrs. Cooper was breading veal chops. "I think *Hercules* would be a good name. He was a hero in Greek mythology who had enormous strength."

"A bicycle should have enormous strength," said Millie. "That's a good suggestion. Thanks." She wrote *Hercules* in her notebook.

Millie was still studying her list when her father came home from work. He took off his hat and coat and handed Millie his copy of the *Chicago Daily News*.

Back in November, Millie couldn't wait to get to the newspaper to check the weather forecast for snow. But right now she was thinking about bicycles and looking forward to spring.

"Shall I turn up the heat?" Mr. Cooper asked when he saw Millie with her earmuffs on. "I wouldn't want you to freeze your ears off."

"I can think better when I wear my earmuffs," said Millie. "Do you happen to have a good name for a bicycle? Mama gave me *Hercules,* but I can enter as many times as I like."

"How about *Atlas*?" her father suggested.

"*Atlas*? Is he the one on our book of maps?

That big guy who's carrying the world on his shoulders?"

"That's the one."

"He'd have to be pretty strong to carry the whole world on his shoulders," Millie observed. "That's a good name, too. Thanks, Daddy."

Millie added the name *Atlas* to her list. She thought of all the kids who were adding bicycle names to their lists and would be entering the contest.

"I don't know," she said as she sat down to eat. "Maybe I shouldn't even bother to enter. What if I lose?"

"There's always a chance of that," said her father. "But if you don't enter, you won't have any chance of winning, either."

Millie thought this over while she chewed a piece of veal. A small chance was better than no chance. And winning a bike would be easier than trying to convince her mother and father to buy her one. She would send in five names. Her own three best ones and the two from her mother and father. One of them just might be the winner.

Millie thought about winning as she took another bite of veal and washed it down with some Old Colony ginger ale. She imagined her bicycle being delivered in a huge truck, while all the neighbors were outside watching and reporters from the radio station were interviewing her.

"And how did you think of so many swell names for bicycles, Millie?"

"Well, my mother and father helped me."

Millie was so busy shaking hands with the reporters and answering their questions that she forgot about taking her earmuffs off until it was time to go to sleep.

The Blue Book
of Songs

February was a very good month. It was one of Millie's favorites, and she had come to look forward to it. There were special days to celebrate—Washington's Birthday, Lincoln's Birthday, and Valentine's Day—and special songs to sing, which always lightened Millie's heart. And happily for Millie, all that celebrating took time away from some of the regular schoolwork that she hated. Like arithmetic and map reading.

Millie especially liked Valentine's Day. In the second grade the teacher had given them a party. The kids had recited valentine poems that they made up themselves, and Millie's mother had baked heart-shaped cinnamon cookies for the whole class.

On Monday Millie sat at her desk making up her valentine list for Valentine's Day on Friday. She looked up and down the rows to make sure that the names on her list matched the kids sitting at their seats. She didn't want to leave anyone out. She wanted to make sure that every kid got at least one valentine.

That's because in first and second grade Millie had observed that the popular kids, like Letty Loeb and Rochelle Liederman, received lots of valentines, while some kids got only one or two. Others, like Thelma Gerch, didn't get any. Thelma sat in the last seat of the last row and never spoke to anyone. Nobody spoke to her either. It was almost as if she were invisible.

Millie was grateful that she wasn't invisible, and that the other kids noticed her. There must have been kids who liked her, because she had gotten quite a few valentines. Not nearly as many as Letty and Rochelle, but enough to make up a reasonable-sized pile.

But Millie knew how bad she would feel if she didn't receive any valentines, or even if she got only one or two. She could just imagine it. They would pass out the valentines and she would be one of those kids who got hardly any. What if the kids who liked her the last two years didn't like her this year? It was possible. Kids changed. They changed best friends all the time. Like Dolores Singer and Natalie Bloom. Last week

11

they took a blood oath to be best friends for life. Now they weren't even talking to each other.

Millie and Sandy Feinman were lucky. They had remained best friends since first grade. And they would be best friends for life, she was sure, even without a blood oath.

Just as Millie was beginning to go over her list once more, Miss Brennan walked up to the front of the room and ordered the class to "Clear your desks for music and take out your *Blue Book of Songs.*"

"I hope she doesn't have us sing about the girdles," Sandy Feinman whispered over her shoulder.

Millie giggled as she put away her list and took out her songbook. One of the songs Miss Brennan sometimes liked to start the music period with had a line that went: ". . . pavilioned in splendor and girded with praise." Whenever they came to the word *girded,* the boys very loudly sang *girdled,* and the whole class went crazy.

The first time that happened, Miss Brennan had explained that the word was not *girdled,* and it had nothing to do with the girdles their mothers wore. The word was *girded.* And it meant "to surround" or "to encircle." But no matter how often she gave that explanation, the boys still sang *girdled.*

Miss Brennan adjusted her wig. She had to do that every so often, because sometimes her hair sat lopsided on her head. "This month we will sing patriotic songs in honor of our presidents' birthdays. And this month, too, we will begin something new. Poetry readings."

Poetry readings? Miss Brennan was going to read poetry to them? Millie was delighted. She bounced up and down in her seat. She had begun to love poetry ever since Thanksgiving, when her mother gave her a book, *A Child's Garden of Verses,* by Robert Louis Stevenson. It was a beautiful book with pictures that looked so real to Millie she could imagine herself in each one of them. It was almost as if she could step inside each scene and become part of the poem. She knew lots of the poems by heart.

O.C. Goodwin and Howard Hall were not delighted. They sat at their desks, groaning.

Miss Brennan gave them one of her cold stares. "Poetry, Mr. Goodwin and Mr. Hall, is not just birds and flowers. There are also poems about wars, shipwrecks, and other disasters."

O.C. Goodwin and Howard Hall looked up with sudden interest.

"Now back to our presidents and our music."

13

Miss Brennan picked up her *Blue Book of Songs.* "On the twelfth of this month we will celebrate the birthday of Abraham Lincoln. Who remembers which war was being fought at the time of Lincoln?"

The Civil War, Millie thought, and almost raised her hand. Or was it the Revolutionary War? Miss Brennan had spoken to them about the two wars when they first began to learn the songs. One war had to do with Lincoln and the other with Washington. But now she wasn't sure which was which. Lots of times she thought she knew the answers to Miss Brennan's questions, but she was afraid to raise her hand.

O.C. Goodwin raised his hand and Miss Brennan called on him. "The Silver War," he said, and the whole class burst out laughing. Then Howard called out, "Hi-yo, Silver," and they laughed even harder. That's exactly what Millie didn't want to happen to her. To be wrong and have everybody laugh at her.

Something like that had happened to her once, at the beginning of the year. She had been reading out loud from the *Weekly Reader,* when she came to a name that she had never seen before. She paused for a moment to figure it out, and when she did, she read what she thought was a very unusual name. "Glad Eyes."

"It's not 'Glad Eyes,' Miss Cooper. It's

14

Gladys, Glad-iss. A third-grader should know that name," Miss Brennan had said.

Not only had the class laughed at her, they had teased her about "Glad Eyes" for over a week.

Now the class was laughing at O.C. Goodwin.

"Not Silver War," Miss Brennan corrected. "Civil War. The war between our Northern States and our Southern States. Between the Yankees in blue and the Confederates in gray. When Americans fought Americans. When brothers turned against brothers." She clasped her hands to her chest and let out a deep sigh.

She should have been an actress, thought Millie. She sounded like Ethel Barrymore on the "Lux Radio Theater."

"So," said Miss Brennan, unclasping her hands, "beginning today and all this week we will be singing songs about that war, and about Abraham Lincoln. But first let's oil our pipes."

Millie hated it when Miss Brennan told them to oil their pipes. The idea of oily pipes inside her body made her feel sick.

"Turn to the bottom of page 132," Miss Brennan said, walking over to the piano, "and we will warm up with a familiar song."

Millie turned to page 132. "Oh, no," she whispered to Sandy, "the girdle song."

Miss Brennan struck a note and hummed

loudly. The class hummed the note with her, and when Miss Brennan was satisfied that everyone was humming on key, she began conducting with her ruler and singing in her opera singer's voice.

The song was called "O Worship the King," and whenever they sang it Millie tried to imagine a king sitting on a throne, while all around people were worshiping him. The class sang with Miss Brennan, ". . . our shield and defender the ancient of days . . ." O.C. Goodwin and Howard Hall were snickering in anticipation ". . . pavilioned in splendor and . . ." Millie clamped her hands over her ears, but she could still hear "girdled with praise." The whole class burst into laughter. Miss Brennan shot them angry looks and struck the ruler against her desk until everyone quieted down.

Next came the expected punishment. "Immediately after music today, you will each write one hundred times, 'I will show respect during music.' Any further outbursts and you will write it five hundred times."

They began the song again, with Miss Brennan accompanying them on the piano, and this time no one sang *girdled.* When they had finished and their pipes were oiled, Miss Brennan reminded them to "sing clearly and crisply.

Loudly, without shouting, and softly, without mumbling." Then, while Miss Brennan played the piano, they went on to sing "When Johnny Comes Marching Home," a song Millie knew from last year and liked because it was bright and cheery. It told about Johnny coming home from the war and everybody coming out to meet him: men, boys, and ladies.

Then they sang, "Just Before the Battle, Mother." It was a sad song about a soldier who tells his mother that they might never see each other again because he might get killed in the war. There was a line in it that sent shivers up Millie's back. "But oh, you'll not forget me mother, if I am numbered with the slain." Millie did not like the word *slain*. They had sung this song only twice before, so Miss Brennan got up from the piano bench and began conducting with her ruler to make sure she could hear everyone singing correctly.

They were on the part that went, "I am thinking most of you," when Miss Brennan substituted the words, "Someone's singing out of tune." She walked up and down the aisles listening carefully to each person's voice until she caught the culprit. Marlene Kaufman. "Miss Kaufman, do not sing," said Miss Brennan. "Just move your lips."

And that's what Marlene did. She moved her lips and only pretended to sing.

Millie thought that was a mean thing for Miss Brennan to do. Everyone should be allowed to sing, even people who couldn't carry a tune. She hoped Marlene's feelings weren't hurt too much. Millie knew that her own feelings would be hurt. I wouldn't move my lips, she thought. I would shut my mouth and never say one word to Miss Brennan.

When they got around to singing "Illinois," Millie cheered up. She thought it was so nice that someone would want to write a whole song about her state, about "thy rivers gently flowing" and "thy prairies verdant growing."

It was a lovely time, singing in a room that felt so warm and peaceful. Millie looked around at the silhouettes of Lincoln and Washington that had been pinned on the window curtains, and she sang, ". . . On the record of thy years, Ab'ram Lincoln's name appears . . ." She loved Abraham Lincoln. He was her favorite president. He was kind and honest and he had freed the slaves.

When the music period was over, the class began working on their punishment assignment. At the beginning of the school year, all the kids had groaned when the punishment assignments were given out. But then they had discovered carbon paper. Using three sheets of carbon paper, and pressing hard on your pencil, you could write the sentence just twenty-five times. The other seventy-five times came out automatically, and Miss Brennan never seemed to notice the difference. The kids knew that she just checked the name on the first page of each assignment to make sure everybody handed it in. And the first page was always the original one.

Millie finished her sentences and went back to her valentine list. She looked at the name *O.C. Goodwin* that she had written down. She would even send one to him. They had been enemies back in 3B, but they had traded comic books, and now in 3A they were almost friends.

Would O.C. send her a valentine? Probably not. Neither would Howard Hall. Not many of the boys had sent them to her last year. Rochelle Liederman and Letty Loeb never sent her any. And she wasn't sure about Dolores Singer or Natalie Bloom. They did in first grade but not in second. Come to think of it, there were lots of kids who wouldn't send her any. The more Millie looked at her list, the more worried she became that nobody—except for Sandy—would send her a valentine. What if she, like Thelma Gerch, suddenly became invisible?

Hot Peppers

"Let's walk slowly," said Millie, adjusting her Mickey Mouse earmuffs. "Give it a chance to rain."

It was lunchtime Tuesday, and Millie and Sandy were going somewhere to eat. Either to Dave's, the hot dog place a block away from school, or home. It all depended on the weather. The snow had melted and rain was forecast.

The walk home from Lawson School was a long one, so whenever it looked like rain, Mrs. Cooper gave Millie money to eat out. Millie loved to eat out, and her mother had given her money today.

She looked up at the sky, at the dark clouds that promised rain. If it didn't rain, she would have to go home. But if it did, it meant eating at Dave's—and hot dogs. She didn't need a thunderstorm. A light drizzle was good enough. Even one drop . . .

"Hey, I think I felt something," said Sandy. "Right on my head." Sandy usually made plans to eat out on rainy days, too.

"Are you sure?" Millie took off her mittens and held her hands out in front of her, palms up, and waited. A drop landed on a finger.

"You're right!" she shouted. "Let's go!" And they ran down Thirteenth Street together, holding hands and laughing.

The aroma of hot dogs and french fries greeted them even before they reached the door, and Millie got hungrier by the second. Dave's was packed with kids from Lawson School. Marlene Kaufman was already there, and so was Angela Moretti, another girl in their class. They were sitting at a table together, eating hot dogs. When they spotted Millie and Sandy, they motioned for them to come over and sit at their table. Millie and Sandy nodded to let them know that they would. But first they went over to the counter to place their orders with Dave and the lady who worked there.

"I'll have a hot dog, loaded," said Sandy.

"And I'll have one with everything on it except hot peppers," said Millie. Millie licked her lips as she watched Dave place a hot dog in a bun and smother it with relish, onions, and pickles. When he saw Millie watching him, he smiled

at her and gave her another slice of pickle. Then
he placed Millie's loaded hot dog onto a thin
sheet of white paper, added a batch of french
fries, and wrapped it all up. She ordered a choco-
late phosphate, paid the cashier a quarter for her
lunch, and carried it over to the table.

"It must be raining out," said Angela Moretti
as Millie sat down.

Angela Moretti wore long braids like Millie
did, and she was very small and thin. "Petite"
was how Millie's mother described her. Millie
knew she could not be described as petite. Neither could Sandy or Marlene. They were the tall-
est girls in the class.

The room was smoky and steamy, so Millie
took off her earmuffs and put them in her coat
pocket. Then she unwrapped her hot dog and
took a bite. Mustard oozed out and dribbled
down her chin. Pieces of onion and relish
dropped onto the paper. It was wonderful. She
would come here for lunch every afternoon if
she could. But she knew that her mother would
never let her eat hot dogs every day. Angela
Moretti ate hot dogs every day. Her mother
worked, and Angela came here every lunch hour
and ate hot dogs. Millie thought that might be
the reason she was so small. Maybe all those hot
dogs kept her from growing.

At a table next to them, a couple of girls were eating hot dogs and signing valentines at the same time.

"Did you make out your valentines already?" Marlene asked, dipping a french fry into some ketchup.

"Ahhh," gasped Sandy. She gulped down some Coke. Her eyes turned red and watery.

"You don't have to get all excited," said Marlene. "There's lots of time left. You still have three days to go."

"Ahhh—it's not the valentines. It's—ahhh—the hot peppers." Sandy dabbed her eyes with a napkin and took another drink.

"You keep doing that," said Millie. "Why do you always order hot peppers when they do that to you?"

"I like them," said Sandy, taking another bite.

"My valentines are all made out," said Marlene. "Except I don't have one to send to Miss Brennan. I wonder if I can find one that says, 'Valentine, will you be mine? Don't tell me. Just move your lips.'"

Millie and Angela burst out laughing, sputtering pieces of onions and relish. Sandy almost choked on another hot pepper.

"She doesn't deserve any valentines," Marlene went on. "She isn't even giving us a party."

"I didn't even buy my valentines yet," said Angela Moretti. "Maybe I'll get them today after school. Oh, I just love Valentine's Day. Don't you?"

Millie stopped eating and looked at the three girls. They would probably send her valentines. Marlene Kaufman had sent her one in the second grade. Angela Moretti hadn't. But they were better friends now. And Sandy would, for sure. But what if that's all she received? Just their three? Three valentines seemed so sad.

Last night Millie had given a lot of thought to the valentine dilemma. She had one of two choices. Choice one: She could send valentines to herself. She knew that some kids in her class did that so they wouldn't get just a few and be embarrassed in front of everyone. She could send herself valentines and sign them "From a Secret Admirer" or "A Friend." But she wasn't sure how she would feel, sending them to herself. She could fool the class, but she couldn't fool herself. Deep down she would know that the valentines didn't count.

Then there was choice two: She could tell everyone not to send her any valentines. They might send her some anyway. But if they didn't, the kids would understand why, and it wouldn't be so sad and embarrassing.

"I hope I get lots of valentines," said Angela.

"You won't get as many as Letty and Rochelle," Marlene told her.

"You won't either. Almost nobody gets as many as Letty and Rochelle."

Suddenly Millie's hot dog didn't taste as good as it had before.

"It doesn't matter how many anyone else gets," said Sandy. "Just so you get enough."

The conversation was making Millie nervous. Her stomach was starting to hurt.

"I'd better hurry up and buy my valentines," said Angela. "I have so many to send."

"I do too," said Marlene.

"Don't send me any valentines," Millie blurted out.

"What?" asked Angela.

"Don't send me any valentines," Millie repeated. She took a small bite of hot dog and chewed slowly.

"Why not?"

"I don't want any."

"Everyone wants valentines," said Sandy. She had given up and left the hot peppers sitting on the paper.

"I don't."

"Why not?"

"Because. I just don't think valentines are such a big deal, that's all." What was she say-

ing? Valentines were a big deal. She loved them.

"Sure they are," said Angela. "They're fun and they're pretty."

"They're okay," said Millie weakly. "Just no big deal."

"There's nothing you can do about it," said Marlene. "People will still send them to you even if you don't want any."

"They won't if I tell them not to." She couldn't believe she had actually said that.

The three girls looked at her, puzzled.

After school Millie helped herself to a tangerine and settled in front of the radio. She listened excitedly while the announcer described the "beautiful blue girl's bicycle, fully equipped with basket and luggage carrier" that she could win in the Name Your Bicycle contest. "The winners will be notified by mail within four weeks after the contest ends," the announcer said. "And the prizewinning entries will be announced over the air."

Millie imagined her name being announced over the air. "And the winner of the beautiful blue, fully equipped girl's bicycle is . . . Millie Cooper—a third-grader at the Victor Lawson Elementary School—with her prizewinning entry, *Hercules.* She imagined him announcing her prizewinning entry five times. Each time she substituted one of her other bicycle names.

Millie ran into the kitchen to check the John Hancock Life Insurance Company calendar hanging on the wall. Four weeks from the end of the contest was March 15. By that time she would know if she had won. She circled the date with a pencil. Then she took out five penny postcards from a kitchen drawer. On each postcard she wrote her name, address, phone number, and one of her bicycle names. She printed the name in capital letters so it would stand out. She would mail the postcards tomorrow, on the way to school.

In that same drawer, Millie found a comic book she had been saving. She was saving it because the whole back cover was an ad, in comic-strip form, for a Schwinn-Built bicycle. It told the story of a boy who saved the day by racing to the train station on his Schwinn-Built bicycle to deliver the briefcase his father had forgotten. The boy made it just in time—only seconds before the train pulled out of the station. Millie loved the ad and read it over and over again.

Millie knew the power of advertising. She read cereal boxes all the time that convinced her to send away for all kinds of swell decoders and amazing magnet or secret-compartment rings.

And back in November she had left a newspaper ad for the new Reynolds Rocket ballpoint pen lying around the house for her mother and father to read. She was sure the ad had helped convince them to buy her the pen.

Millie decided to leave the comic book out. She wanted her mother and father to read the ad and see how important it was to have a bicycle, especially a Schwinn-Built. If Millie had one, then she could save the day for her father. He didn't carry a briefcase, and he never went anywhere— except to work at his furniture factory—but a bicycle would be handy to have around, just in case. What if one day he suddenly ran out of furniture polish? Millie could race over to Woolworth's on her Schwinn-Built, buy the polish, and save the day by delivering it to the factory just in time.

Throughout the evening, Millie planted the comic book, back cover up, in all the important places around the apartment. On top of the kitchen table so her mother would see it when she cleared the table for supper. Near the radio so her mother and father could read it and listen to their programs at the same time. And later on, in the bathroom.

As a further hint, she sang "A Bicycle Built for Two" as she got ready for bed. It was the only bicycle song she could think of. She sang it clearly and crisply. And loudly, without shouting:

> It won't be a stylish marriage
> I can't afford a carriage
> But you'll look sweet
> Upon the seat
> Of a BICYCLE built for two.

Valentine's Day

"Some Valentine's Day this is going to be," Millie said to herself as she walked into the classroom on Friday. "No party, and probably no valentines either." She had made sure to tell as many kids as she could not to send her any valentines. And when they said things like "You don't mean it, do you?" Marlene Kaufman seemed to feel the need to defend Millie by answering "Sure she does." Now Millie wished that both she and Marlene had kept their mouths shut. She wished she were absent.

Angela Moretti was absent. Maybe she was worried about not getting enough valentines too.

"Angela Moretti is in the hospital," Miss Brennan announced at the end of silent reading. "She's having her appendix out."

All the kids looked up from their books and made *ooh*ing and *aah*ing sounds. No one in their

32

class had ever been in the hospital before. And having an appendix out sounded very important.

"I'll bet it's from all those hot dogs," Millie told Sandy.

Sandy turned around to look at Millie. "I think she should start eating cheese sandwiches from now on."

"I had my appendix out when I was three," said Millie. "I had an acute case." Millie remembered hearing about her acute case of appendicitis—which meant that she had to have an emergency operation—and how she had gone around telling people she had a cute case.

"I know," said Sandy. "You told me yours came from monkey-nut shells."

Millie pictured the tiny nuts in their hard, tan-colored shells. Her father had bought them for her from the "nut man" who sold all kinds of nuts at an outdoor stand on Roosevelt Road. Millie had to crack the shells with her teeth to get at the nuts, and it was hard to do. The nuts and pieces of shell got all mixed up together. The next day Millie had a terrible stomachache that turned out to be appendicitis. Her doctor said it had something to do with the monkey-nut shells.

"Angela had an acute case of appendicitis and will be out for a couple of weeks," Miss Brennan continued. "But her mother will deliver her valentines to Angela in the hospital. So pass your valentines for her up to the front of the room. Miss Feinman, you may collect them."

Millie found her valentine to Angela and gave it to Sandy. While Sandy was collecting Angela's valentines from the front desks, Miss Brennan took a large box out of the closet. It was covered with dingy white crepe paper and decorated with red crepe-paper hearts. The box looked as if it had seen many years' worth of Valentine's Days. Miss Brennan set it on a small table, next to the globe of the world.

"Now you may pass the rest of your valentines up to the front, and the person in the first seat of each row will deposit them in our valentine box."

Millie passed hers up and watched while the kids collected all the valentines and put them in the box. She wondered if any of those valentines were for her. She hoped that lots of them were, and that nobody had paid attention to her request for no valentines. But even if they had listened to her, she was protected. People wouldn't say that nobody wanted to send Millie Cooper any valentines. They would just say that Millie didn't want any.

At two forty-five Miss Brennan looked at the clock and announced, "We will allow fifteen min-

34

utes to pass out the valentines, and you may look at them until it's time to go home."

That's all there was to Valentine's Day in Miss Brennan's room. Millie wished there would be a party like the one in second grade. Everybody would be so busy eating cookies they wouldn't pay much attention to the number of valentines each kid got.

"I will choose two people—one boy and one girl—to be messengers," Miss Brennan went on. "If you want to be picked, you must sit up straight and tall with your hands folded. I don't want to see any hand-waving."

The entire class sat up so straight and stiff, it looked as if they'd all taken a bath in laundry starch. Millie folded her hands tightly on her desk and stretched herself upward. If she could be a messenger, then maybe no one would notice how many valentines she received.

Miss Brennan eyed her thirty-five students, frozen in place. "Mr. Simon, you may come up, and Miss . . ."

Millie shut her eyes and made a silent plea, *Oh, please pick me, just this once, please . . .*

"Miss Liederman, you may come up."

A jubilant Freddie Simon and Rochelle Liederman jumped out of their seats, while the rest of the class sighed and went limp. Millie slumped in her seat. Her only hope for having her number of valentines go unnoticed was lost.

Freddie and Rochelle pulled handfuls of valentines from the box. They argued for a moment about who had taken too many, and then they began their delivery.

Millie watched as they made their way up and down the aisles, passing out valentines and trying to avoid being tripped by O.C. Goodwin and Howard Hall. Millie had heard O.C. threaten to beat up any kid who didn't send him a valentine, so he was getting lots. So were Letty Loeb and Dolores Singer. Millie could see envelopes piling up on their desks. Even Marlene Kaufman was receiving lots of valentines. And Sandy, too. Millie tried not to watch, but she could still hear the slapping of valentines on desks all around her, and the delighted squeals that followed.

Then there were the few kids who weren't getting any. Kids like Myra Glass, who had stringy hair and always looked a little gray, as though she never took a bath; and Elmer Bass, who was kind of goofy, always laughing, even when there was nothing to laugh at. They were waiting, hoping for at least one valentine. And one would eventually come—from Millie. Millie waited and hoped too, but she wasn't getting any. Not a single one. Never had she felt so alone. There were

thirty-five students in her class, but she felt as if she were sitting in the room invisible, like Thelma Gerch.

Rochelle picked out two valentines from her dwindling pile and started walking toward her. At last! Millie straightened up and smiled at Rochelle. But Rochelle walked right past her.

Millie suddenly felt the need to do something. To rearrange the books in her desk. To check the inkwell to see if it needed refilling. Anything was better than facing the class, looking as if she cared. If this had happened to her in 3B, she would have cried. But now she was in 3A, and she was able to hold back the tears. She couldn't believe that nobody had sent her a valentine. Someone should have. She had asked the kids not to. But they didn't have to listen to her, did they?

She read and reread the initials carved on the top of her desk: CB, MH, LS. She was tracing the letters CB with her finger when, from out of the air, an envelope dropped in front of her. Millie's name, in tiny letters, was written on the front. She recognized the handwriting.

"I hope you're not mad at me for giving it to you."

Millie looked up from her desk. Sandy had turned around in her seat and was facing her. "I know you said you didn't want any, but I decided to give you one anyway."

"I'm not mad," said Millie, opening the envelope and pulling out the card. "This one is really nice."

The valentine was cut out in the shape of a girl who was looking into a heart-shaped mirror, on which the words *Valentine, who loves you?* were written. When Millie pulled out the tab, another girl's face appeared in the mirror, with the words, *I DO!*

The mirror reminded Millie of the story of Snow White, in which the wicked queen looked into her mirror and asked, "Mirror, mirror, on the wall, who's the fairest one of all?"

"This is really nice," Millie repeated. She tucked the valentine inside her dress pocket and looked around the room while she waited for the bell to ring. She studied all the pictures of George Washington and Abraham Lincoln that were hanging up. None of the pictures showed them smiling. Come to think of it, she had never seen George Washington or Abraham Lincoln smiling. But that was okay. She wasn't smiling either.

Things Pick Up

Millie took the valentine out of her pocket and placed it on top of the dresser next to her copy of *A Child's Garden of Verses.* As she stared at the valentine, her mind wandered back over the last few days, to the way it could have been, to all the valentines she could have received and to the way she would have arranged them on her dresser. She was so lost in her thoughts that she didn't hear her mother come into the room.

"What a cute valentine," said Mrs. Cooper. She stood next to Millie and put an arm around her shoulder. "Is this your favorite one?"

Millie looked up into her mother's face and their eyes met. "It's my only one," she said.

Mrs. Cooper picked up the valentine and fiddled with the tab, making the girl in the mirror appear and disappear. "I see it's from Sandy. She really is a best friend, isn't she?"

"She's my only friend," said Millie, and she

dropped herself onto her bed and picked up a pillow to hug.

Mrs. Cooper sat down next to her. "You didn't get any other valentines?"

"No." Millie shook her head.

"Well, things like this happen sometimes." Her mother moved closer to Millie.

"But it's my own fault," said Millie, and she went on to tell the whole awful story. She told it all in one breath.

"I was afraid I wouldn't be getting too many valentines and I didn't want to be embarrassed so I told everyone not to send me any so I would have an excuse but I didn't want them to listen to me but they did." Millie felt her lower lip begin to quiver.

Her mother was very quiet for a moment, and Millie could tell by the look on her face that she was trying to get the story clear in her mind.

"Tillie Lesh," said Mrs. Cooper after a while.

"What," asked Millie, "is a Tillie Lesh?"

"Tillie Lesh," Mrs. Cooper explained, "is not a what. She was a who. When I was in eighth grade, Tillie Lesh had a party. It was the first boy-girl party I ever went to, and I was so excited about it. At the party the boys stood off in one corner and the girls were in another, waiting to be asked to dance. One by one the boys would come over and ask the girls to dance. And I was afraid that I wouldn't be asked, and I'd be humiliated standing in the corner all by myself. So I ran off and hid in the bathroom for most of the evening. And I never got to dance—not even once."

"Oh, Mama, that's awful," said Millie, taking her mother's hand and trying to comfort her. "But maybe you would've been asked. Maybe you would've danced all night."

"Maybe. I'll never know. I was so afraid to take the chance of being hurt, that I spoiled my chance to have a good time."

"Like me with the valentines," said Millie. "I spoiled my chances of getting valentines."

Her mother nodded. "And the bike contest, remember? If you want to win, you have to risk losing. Sometimes it's easier to play it safe and not take chances. But if we always did that, life wouldn't be very interesting or satisfying, would it?"

Millie shook her head. Taking a chance with the bike contest had been easy. But taking a chance with the valentines had seemed so hard.

"Now come on." Mrs. Cooper patted Millie's shoulder and got up from the bed. "How about a game of Authors or Rummy before supper?"

"Maybe later," said Millie. "I want to think first."

After her mother left, Millie sat on her bed,

hugging her pillow and thinking over the things her mother had said. A person had to take chances. She remembered taking a chance once—when she was in the first grade.

It happened on the first day of school. Millie and Sandy were in the same class, but they hadn't met. Then during recess, Millie saw Sandy sitting on a swing, singing to herself. For some reason, Millie knew that she would like to be friends with Sandy. She wanted to go up to her and ask her if she would like a push on the swing. But she was afraid. What if Sandy said no? Or told her to go away? Millie remembered how she had gathered all her courage and walked right up to Sandy and asked, "Want a push?"

"Yeah, push me high," Sandy had said.

After Sandy had been swinging for a while, she pushed Millie. But Millie got dizzy after just one swing. They both laughed about it, and they became friends then. And after that, best friends. Thinking about it now, Millie understood that if she hadn't taken that chance with Sandy, she might have missed out on their friendship.

Millie heard a key turn in the front door. She tossed the pillow onto the bed and ran to meet her father.

"You're home from work," said Millie, reaching up for a kiss.

"And no work for a whole weekend," her father said, smiling at her and handing her the newspaper.

"No thanks, Daddy. I don't think I care about the weather anymore." She turned away, but then turned back. "Well, I do care about Li'l Abner and Dotty Dripple."

"And I bet there's something else in the paper that you'll care about."

"What?" asked Millie, jumping up and down.

"See for yourself."

Millie ran into the dining room and spread the paper out on the table. She began turning the pages. There were the usual store ads for Marshall Field's and The Fair, and there were the comics, and lots of car ads for the new 1947 Kaiser and Packard and Buick. And American Airlines was advertising a nonstop flight to Los Angeles in just seven and a half hours. But there was nothing that she cared about. She turned a few more pages. And then she saw it!

Win a Bike!
Boys and Girls!
Get Ready for Spring!
Sell 20 Subscriptions to the *Chicago Daily News*
and Win a Fully Equipped Bicycle!

"I found it!" Millie called out. "This is what you meant, isn't it, Daddy? The subscriptions and the bicycle?"

"What is this about subscriptions and bicycles?" Mrs. Cooper asked, coming into the dining room with Mr. Cooper.

"Look," Millie said, showing her mother the ad. "All I have to do is sell twenty subscriptions to the *Daily News* and I can win a bike."

Millie began to read out loud. " 'A fully equipped streamlined tank model that rides like a million. It has balloon tires and tubes; a luggage carrier, safe, trouble-free coaster brakes, and a sturdy kickstand. Boys' models and girls' models. Your choice of red or blue.'

"Blue!" Millie cried out. "I'll pick blue. All I have to do is sell twenty subscriptions."

"Nineteen," Mr. Cooper corrected her.

Millie looked at her father. "Nineteen?" she asked, puzzled. But then she could tell by his expression that he was going to subscribe. He was going to be her first customer!

"You want a subscription?" she asked to be sure.

"Well, why not? I'm getting tired of lugging the paper home every day. And besides, I don't always have a nickel on me, and I hate to bother with getting change."

Millie knew that her father was making it all up. She knew that he really liked to buy the paper when it came out in the late afternoon, and read parts of it at work.

46

"And for a change I'll be able to read the paper first—while all the pages are in order," said Mrs. Cooper, who was always the last one to read it.

"Do you think Uncle Jake or Uncle Joe would want a subscription?" Millie asked.

"I hate to impose on relatives," said Mrs. Cooper. "They might feel obligated to buy the paper even if they don't want to. Maybe you could try to sell subscriptions in the neighborhood, and if you're short by two, we'll ask them."

Millie ran into the kitchen and returned with a pencil and a pair of scissors. She cut out the five subscription blanks that were printed on the page. There was a phone number that she could call for the rest when she needed them. Then she began to fill out one of the forms, writing her parents' names and address on the dotted lines, in her best handwriting. Her father signed it. It was very official-looking.

Millie took out the page that announced the offer, so she could save it with her subscription forms. She looked at everything over and over again all evening.

When it was time for bed, Millie placed the ad and subscription forms on her dresser next to Sandy's valentine. She picked up the valentine and played with the tab, smiling at the girl who smiled back at her. It really was an especially nice valentine.

She flopped onto her bed and sat there, hugging her pillow, happy that the day had ended better than it had begun and pleased that there was so much to look forward to. She had already entered a bike contest, she was going to sell subscriptions, and from now on she would take chances that would make her life more interesting and satisfying. Things were picking up.

"The Charge
of the Light Brigade"

"I don't suppose your mother and father
would want to subscribe to the *Daily News,*" Millie said to Sandy walking to school on Monday.
"I'm selling subscriptions to win a bike."

"We already subscribe to the *Trib,*" said
Sandy.

"The *Trib*? Really? I thought you were Demo-
crats."

"We are."

"I thought only Republicans read the *Tribune.*"

"Well, we read the *Trib* and we're Demo-
crats." Sandy shifted her schoolbag to her other
hand. Her hands were beet red because she
wasn't wearing any mittens. She had to warm
them, one at a time, in her pockets. Millie was
wearing her mittens and her earmuffs. She felt
cozy.

"If you don't win a bike you can always use mine," Sandy offered. When Sandy's cousin Elaine had begun high school last fall, she had given Sandy her bike. She thought that a high schooler was too old to be riding one.

"Thanks," said Millie. "But borrowing a bike isn't like having your own. And besides, I thought we'd ride around together."

They walked along silently in the gentle snowfall, blowing out puffs of air and pretending it was smoke. The smoke reminded Millie of the day last fall when Sandy came riding over to her house on what used to be Elaine's bike. Millie's Uncle Jake was visiting, and he offered to teach Millie how to ride. He ran around the block with her, his cigarette dangling from his mouth, holding on to the seat of the bike to balance her as she pedaled. Millie remembered how she had been riding along, confident that Uncle Jake was right with her.

"How am I doing?" she had asked as she pedaled. When there was no answer, Millie turned around to see her uncle walking far behind her, almost a block away. She fell off the bike. But when she got back on, she knew how to ride.

Millie blew out one last puff as she went into the school and climbed the stairs to Room 210. The morning started out the usual way. The class said the pledge and sang the national anthem. Miss Brennan took attendance and collected milk-and-cookie money. But then, instead of asking the kids to take out their readers, Miss Brennan stood in front of the room and stared at them. She had a mean, fierce look on her face.

Millie and the rest of the class were used to seeing Miss Brennan with mean, fierce looks. But never before had they seen her looking meaner or fiercer. Something was wrong. Millie wondered what they had done to put Miss Brennan in such a bad mood. Everyone was quiet.

Suddenly Miss Brennan shouted out, "Forward the Light Brigade! Charge for the guns!" She flung her arms in all directions. "Boldly they rode and well, into the jaws of Death, into the Mouth of Hell."

The class gasped. They couldn't believe what Miss Brennan was saying. Was she going mad? In total disbelief they listened as she continued:

> Cannon to right of them,
> Cannon to left of them,
> Cannon behind them
>   Volley'd and thunder'd;
> Storm'd at with shot and shell,
> While horse and hero fell,
> They that had fought so well

Came thro' the jaws of Death,
Back from the mouth of Hell,
All that was left of them,
Left of six hundred.

Miss Brennan took a deep breath and became herself again. "Those lines are from a poem by Alfred, Lord Tennyson," she said, looking straight at O.C. Goodwin and Howard Hall, who stared back at her with their mouths open. "He was an English poet who was born in 1809, the same year as Abraham Lincoln. And he wrote about a battle in 1854 between the English and the Russians. The English made an attack on a Russian position, and that is what this poem is about."

Miss Brennan took a book from her desk and, while O.C. Goodwin and Howard Hall sat on the edge of their seats, she went on to read the entire poem called "The Charge of the Light Brigade."

After she finished, O.C. Goodwin called out, "What kind of lights did the Light Brigade use? Flashlights?"

Some of the kids laughed, but others didn't. They evidently thought that there was a strong possibility that the Light Brigade did use flashlights.

Millie didn't think they used flashlights.

Flashlights probably weren't invented by 1854. Probably they used lanterns or flaming torches. She had seen movies where men riding horses carried flaming torches so they could go around burning down houses and villages. She wondered if she should raise her hand for the answer. Freddie Simon beat her to it.

"Torches," Freddie said. "They used fiery torches against the Russians."

Miss Brennan shook her head. "The Light Brigade had nothing to do with flashlights or torches. It was the unit of six hundred soldiers mentioned in the poem. The English army also had a Heavy Brigade, which was made up of nine hundred soldiers."

So the Light Brigade had nothing to do with lights. Millie gave a sigh of relief. She was glad she hadn't raised her hand after all.

"Now," said Miss Brennan, placing the book on her desk, "on Friday I want you each to bring in a book with your favorite poem. And for the next several weeks, we will take turns reading them in front of the class."

Millie stiffened. What was Miss Brennan talking about? *She* was supposed to read the poems to the class. Before, she never said anything about the kids reading them. Millie was used to reading her Robert Louis Stevenson poems out loud. Many times she even recited them in front of her mother and father, and to herself. But reading in front of the whole class? Getting criticized by Miss Brennan in front of everyone if she doesn't like the way you're reading, or if you make a mistake?

"What if we don't have a favorite poem?" O.C. Goodwin asked.

"Then you will go to the library and find one," was Miss Brennan's answer.

"I don't have a favorite poem," said Sandy on the way home from school. "And I don't feel like going to the library to get one."

"I'll give you one of mine," said Millie. For Millie, finding a poem to read was easy. There were so many of them that she loved. But reading the poem in front of the class was something else. She didn't know if she could do it.

Selling
Subscriptions

Millie stood in front of Mrs. Golub's door. She had a pencil in one hand and the subscription blanks in the other. Mrs. Golub lived on the first floor, right across from Millie's apartment. Once, when Millie was younger, she had stayed with Mrs. Golub while her mother went to the dentist. Millie remembered spending much of the morning eating and drinking Fig Newtons and Ovaltine.

Mrs. Golub was a nice lady, and as far as Millie knew, she didn't have a paper delivered. She would probably want a subscription. But if she wanted a subscription, wouldn't she have subscribed already?

There was only one way to find out. Millie would have to ask her. Mrs. Golub wouldn't yell at her. But what if she said no? Millie could almost hear her mother and father saying, "You have to take the chance of her saying no, in order to give her the chance to say yes."

Millie put her ear to the door. It was very quiet on the other side. Come to think of it, Mrs. Golub always had her radio on. Millie listened carefully. There was no radio playing. Nothing. It was obvious that Mrs. Golub wasn't home. Relieved, Millie began walking up the stairs to the second floor.

This time she was in front of Mrs. Rissman's apartment. Mrs. Rissman was the youngest lady in the building, and the only one who wore slacks. All the other ladies wore flowered housedresses and aprons. Millie put her ear to the door and listened. It was quiet. Maybe no one was home here either. Millie tapped on the door lightly. Very lightly. Mrs. Rissman had a new baby boy. He might be taking a nap, and Millie wouldn't want to wake him. Then he'd cry, and for sure Mrs. Rissman wouldn't want to buy a subscription. She gave one last tap and walked across to Mrs. Chisever's apartment.

She could hear the sounds of pots and pans clanking, and she could smell food cooking. Millie didn't know Mrs. Chisever that well. What if she yelled at Millie for bothering her while she was cooking supper? Selling subscriptions was not as easy as she had thought it would be the other night. Millie turned and walked up to the third floor.

Standing in front of Mr. Diamond's door, Millie was determined. This time she would knock, and knock loudly. She raised her hand, but in midair stopped. Mr. Diamond was old, and his wife had died just last month. It wouldn't be right to impose. What if he didn't have enough money for a subscription? What if—?

Without warning, the door opened and Millie found her fist in front of Mr. Diamond's face.

"Millie! What a surprise!"

"Oh, hi, Mr. Diamond."

"I was just on my way out. Can I help you?"

"I can come back later," said Millie.

"What is it that you wanted?"

"Well, I was just . . . uh . . . I don't suppose you would want a subscription to the *Daily News*?"

"I already subscribe," said Mr. Diamond, "to the *Tribune*."

"Oh," said Millie, turning to leave and wondering if Mr. Diamond was a Republican. "Thanks anyway." She walked across the hall to the apartment of Mr. and Mrs. Julius Fink. Millie knew them the least of all the neighbors on her side of the building.

Sometimes Mrs. Fink said hello to Millie when they passed each other in the hallway. Mr. Fink usually just grunted. As she stood in front of the door getting ready to knock, Millie tried to be more determined than ever. She had actually asked Mr. Diamond to subscribe, and that hadn't been too bad. She would ask the Finks too. What was the worst that could happen? They would say no, and Millie would go home. It was getting late anyway, and this was the last apartment in this part of the building.

Millie knocked loudly and hoped Mrs. Fink would be the one to answer. Instead she found herself face to face with Mr. Fink. He had a cigar in his mouth and was wearing a pair of pants and an undershirt. Millie's father would never answer the door in an undershirt.

Mr. Fink took the cigar out of his mouth. It was all spitty at one end.

"What is it that you want, girlie?" he asked.

Millie glanced away from the spitty cigar and showed him her subscription forms. "Would you like to subscribe to the *Daily News*? Then you can get the paper delivered and not have to go out to buy it." She waited for an answer while something that felt like Mexican jumping beans danced the jitterbug in her stomach.

"What do I want with a paper?" he asked, pushing away the forms. "Nothin' in it but bad news. Bad enough I gotta hear it on the radio. Polio epidemics, kidnappings, snowstorms, all those men getting lost at the South Pole . . ." He

59

gave Millie an angry look, as if he were blaming her for all that bad news.

"There's good things in there, too," said Millie, thinking of the movie directory and the comic strips.

"Name me one," said Mr. Fink. "Name me one good thing in the paper."

"Well, there's Li'l Abner and Dotty Dripple."

Mr. Fink shook his head. "Sorry, girlie, but I ain't buying' a paper for a couple comic strips." He closed the door in Millie's face.

Millie ran down the three flights of stairs and didn't stop until she came to her apartment. She couldn't wait to get inside, where people spoke nicely to her and didn't hurt or insult her. The subscriptions would have to wait until tomorrow. Or maybe next week.

"How did it go? Any luck?" Mrs. Cooper looked up from the dining room table, where she and Mr. Cooper were discussing the furniture factory.

"I still have nineteen to go," said Millie, showing her mother and father the empty subscription blanks.

"The first time selling is always the hardest," said her father. "It gets easier as you get used to it. Take my salesman, for instance. Couldn't sell anything in the beginning. I thought I'd go out

of business because of him. But he got better. And he gets better all the time. Oh, speaking of sales"—Mr. Cooper slapped his knee—"we signed a new contract today."

Millie sat on the dining room couch, half listening to the radio and half listening to her parents' conversation. She didn't understand most of what they were talking about. But what she did understand gave her an idea.

After supper Millie took a sheet of paper and wrote:

I will get Millie a bike tomorrow.

Underneath that she drew two lines. She brought the paper and a fountain pen over to her mother, who was at the dining room table, working on a crossword puzzle in the newspaper.

"Here," she said, "please sign this." She covered the words with her hand.

Mrs. Cooper looked at Millie and smiled. Then she signed her name on one of the blank lines.

Millie took the pen and paper to her father, who was at the radio, changing stations.

"Would you sign this please?" she asked, covering up the words again.

"What is it?"

"A contract," said Millie. "Just sign your name on the line."

"I can't read what I'm signing," said Mr. Cooper. "You should never sign anything without reading and understanding it first."

"Mama signed it. See?" Millie pointed to her mother's signature.

"Well, if your mother signed it . . . and I've already signed one contract today . . . I guess it can't hurt to sign another."

Millie waited until her father finished writing his name, and then she pulled the paper away. "Aha, gotcha!" she said, showing them what she had written. Her mother and father laughed when they read it.

"I guess I get a bike tomorrow, huh? It says so right here. And you signed it."

"It says tomorrow," said Mrs. Cooper. "And tomorrow, it will still say tomorrow. And after that there will be yet another tomorrow." She laughed again.

"Oh, nuts." Millie considered putting the date on the paper, but decided it wouldn't do any good. They weren't taking her contract seriously anyway.

"More nuts," she said, crumpling the paper and going into her bedroom. She took her *Child's Garden of Verses* from the dresser and lay down on the bed. She read through the poems, trying to decide which one to write for Miss Brennan. "My Shadow" was one of her favorites:

I have a little shadow
    that goes in and out with me,
And what can be the use of him
    is more than I can see.
He is very, very like me
    from the heels up to the head,
And I see him jump before me,
    when I jump into my bed . . .

But she also loved "The Lamplighter," which told of Leerie the lamplighter, who lit the street-lamps every night; Leerie, with his lantern and ladder, posting—not walking—but posting (like a postman?) up the street, lighting the lamps, and making the night safe for boys and girls and their families.

My tea is nearly ready
    and the sun has left the sky,
It's time to take the window
    to see Leerie going by;
For every night at tea-time
    and before you take your seat,
With lantern and with ladder
    he comes posting up the street!

Millie didn't know which poem to choose. But she didn't have to make up her mind right away. She had until Friday to decide.

When Millie went to bed that night, she curled up under the quilt and closed her eyes. She dreamed of the lamplighter walking up and down Thirteenth Street, lighting the streetlamps one by one. And the words of the poem drifted in and out of her dreams:

> For we are very lucky
>   with a lamp before the door,
> And Leerie stops to light it
>   as he lights so many more;
> And O! before you hurry by
>   with ladder and with light,
> O Leerie, see a little child
>   and nod to him tonight!

A Visit to Angela

"How many of you remembered to bring in your favorite poems?" Miss Brennan asked on Friday.

Everyone raised a hand. Even Sandy, who was waiting for Millie to give her one.

"I want you all to copy your poems exactly as they are written in your books," Miss Brennan went on. "I want all the spelling and punctuation to be correct, and they must be written in your best handwriting."

Millie had decided to do "The Lamplighter." It seemed to her that there was something almost mysterious about the poem. Even the name, Leerie, added magic. Millie wondered if Stevenson's lamplighter was named Leerie? Or did he choose that name because it sounded so good with the word *lamplighter*? Leerie the lamplighter. Or was Leerie short for O'Leary? Like Mrs.

O'Leary, whose cow kicked over a lantern in the barn and maybe started the Chicago fire?

Millie gave Sandy her book so she could pick out a favorite poem. "I'm doing 'The Lamplighter,' " Millie told Sandy. "But 'My Shadow' is another one of my favorites. You can have that one if you want."

"I'll take it," said Sandy.

Millie didn't need the book to copy her poem. Not only did she know "The Lamplighter" by heart, but she had read it so many times she could see a picture of the page, exactly as it was printed, in her mind. If only she could just write the poem and not have to read it.

The class copied their poems quietly, except for a few kids who grumbled about how their poems were too long, and how they should have picked shorter ones.

When everyone was finished, Miss Brennan collected the papers. "I will look these over on the weekend, and beginning Monday we will read them out loud."

Out loud! The words struck terror in Millie's heart. How would she ever be able to stand up in front of the whole class and read her poem? In front of a class that would laugh, and a teacher who would make embarrassing comments? It was one thing for Miss Brennan to write private comments on assignments: "Write neater." Or, "Answer questions in full sentences." But to say things to you—"It's not Glad Eyes, Miss Cooper. A third-grader should know that name"—in front of everybody. That was different.

During the afternoon, Millie was able to put the poetry problem out of her mind. They had music and sang songs about George Washington. From *The Blue Book of Songs* they sang "Yankee Doodle" and "Hail, Columbia!"—patriotic songs that mentioned Washington's name. Then they wrote get-well letters to Angela Moretti, who was home from the hospital. Millie and Sandy volunteered to deliver them on the way home from school.

Angela lived in an apartment building next to the Old Colony Bottling Company. Millie thought that Angela was lucky to be living right next door to a famous soda pop company. Sometimes Millie and Sandy stopped there to pick up pieces of dry ice, and see how long they could hold them before the ice started to burn their hands. Millie didn't know what Old Colony did with the dry ice, but there were usually boxes of it in the alley behind the factory. And the Old Colony workers always let the kids take a few pieces if they wanted some.

Angela's grandmother, who was staying with

Angela while her mother was at work, let them in and showed them the way to the bedroom. Angela was sitting in her bed, propped up against a pillow. She was dressing her paper dolls. Her face brightened when she saw Millie and Sandy.

"Hi," said Millie. "We brought you letters from school."

"We did them for today's written composition," Sandy added.

"Oh, good," said Angela. "I'm so bored." She took the letters and put them on her night table. "I'll read them the next time I have nothing to do."

Millie and Sandy sat down on the edge of Angela's bed. "Does it hurt from your operation?" Millie asked.

"Only when I move. Do you want to see where they stitched me up?"

Millie had her own scar that she could look at whenever she wanted to. And she wasn't sure how she felt about looking at someone else's. "Maybe some other time," she said.

"No thanks," said Sandy, making a face. "Did you get our valentines?"

"Yes," said Angela. "But I never even got to make mine out."

Millie wondered if Angela would have sent her one. "What hospital were you in?" she asked.

"Mount Sinai," said Angela.

"Hey, that's where I had mine out," said Millie.

"And I was born there, too," said Angela.

"So was I," said Sandy.

Millie was happy to see how much they all had in common. "I was born in Garfield Park."

Angela's eyes widened. "You were born in the park?"

Millie laughed. "Not the park. The hospital. Garfield Park Hospital."

"That's better," said Angela.

Millie and Sandy stayed a few more minutes, and then they left for home. They considered stopping at Old Colony for dry ice but decided to wait until summer, when it was warmer.

When Millie reached her apartment building, she looked through the slits in the mailbox to see if there were any letters. The box was empty. She was hoping that something might have come from the bicycle contest. It had been only one week since the contest ended, but maybe the people liked Millie's entries so much, they didn't have to take a whole month to reach a decision.

Millie rang the bell and her mother let her in. The whole apartment smelled from the chicken and soup that were cooking. The kitchen floor was covered with newspapers, the way it was every Friday after her mother washed the floor. The newspapers kept the floor clean.

"Did anything come for me in the afternoon mail?" Millie asked as she opened the refrigerator door to get a tangerine. She already knew that the morning mail didn't bring anything but bills and advertisements.

"Nothing but bills and advertisements," said Mrs. Cooper, who was at the sink washing some blouses in Rinso and singing, "Rinso white, Rinso bright, happy little washday song."

Millie thought it was dumb the way soap companies made up songs so people would think it was fun to do the laundry. She peeled the tangerine and popped sections of it into her mouth. "I can't wait to find out about the bike contest. I really do want a bike."

"You can always sell those subscriptions," her mother reminded her.

"I tried, and it didn't work out right."

"Maybe you can give it another chance in a few days."

Chance. There was that word again.

"Daddy will be home soon," said Mrs. Cooper, squeezing water out of a blouse. "How about picking up the papers for me?"

"Sure." Millie threw her tangerine peel away and began picking up the papers. One page—a bicycle ad—caught her attention, and she stopped to read it.

BICYCLES FOR THE WHOLE FAMILY!
Mom Can Discard Her Girdle
and Keep Her Girlish Figure.
Dad Can Bicycle His Way to a Healthy Tan.
And Junior Can Go on Long Rides
with the Gang.

A wonderful ad, Millie thought. And a whole new approach. Not only should a child have a bicycle, so should a mother and father.

Millie threw all the other papers away. But this one she left for her mother to see. Right there in the middle of the kitchen floor.

I Never Saw
a Purple Cow

"Who would like to be the first to read their poem out loud?" Miss Brennan asked. She was standing in front of the class, holding the pile of written poems in both hands.

Millie avoided Miss Brennan's gaze and looked around the room. Almost everyone, it seemed, was trying to avoid Miss Brennan's gaze.

"Do we have to read?" O.C. Goodwin asked.

"I expect you all to read," said Miss Brennan, "but I will not force anyone."

Sighs of relief could be heard throughout the room. Millie's sigh was the deepest of all. She didn't have to read. She felt the way she thought Atlas would feel if he were told that he could take the day off from carrying the world around on his shoulders. She couldn't believe her good luck. She could just sit back and relax and listen to the others.

"I thought it would be nice to start each day

with the reading of two or three poems," said Miss Brennan, placing the papers in a wooden box on top of her desk. "And we will continue until everyone who wants to read gets the chance."

She moved her chair over to a window and sat down. "Do I have any volunteers?" she asked.

The class was silent.

"Does anyone here want to do us the honor of being first?"

"I'll do the honor," said O.C. Goodwin, jumping to his feet.

"Very well then, Mr. Goodwin, you may come forward and find your poem in the box."

O.C. looked through the pile until he found his poem. Then he turned to face the class and grinned.

"Now I want you to stand up straight and tall," Miss Brennan instructed, "and tell us the title of the poem, and the name of the poet."

" 'The Purple Cow,' " O.C. announced. "By Gelett Burgess." O.C. put the paper up in front of his face and began reading. It sounded like he had a pillow over his face. Millie couldn't understand a word he was saying. Neither could Miss Brennan.

"Don't mumble, Mr. Goodwin. Speak up. Pronounce your words slowly and clearly."

Millie knew she'd hate to be in O.C.'s place,

with Miss Brennan telling her not to mumble.

"Now try again," said Miss Brennan. "And this time, take the paper away from your face."

O.C. cleared his throat and grinned at the class again. Then he began:

> I never saw a purple cow,
> I never hope to see one;
> But I can tell you anyhow,
> I'd rather see than be one.

When he was finished, Millie and the rest of the class applauded and O.C. took a bow. Some of the kids made mooing sounds.

"That, class, is Mr. Goodwin's favorite poem. Who else has a favorite poem?"

"It's not my favorite," O.C. corrected her as he went back to his seat. "But it was the shortest one I could find."

Miss Brennan rolled her eyes upward. "Who else would like to volunteer?"

Howard Hall, wanting to do the honor of being second, shot his hand up in the air.

Miss Brennan seemed pleased. "Mr. Hall, you may come up."

Howard Hall took his poem from the box and faced the class. "The title of my poem is 'If All the World Were Paper,' and it was written by Anon. But I don't know if that's his first name or his last name." Some of the kids giggled.

Millie couldn't see what was so funny. She didn't know if it was a first or last name either.

"Anon is an abbreviation for the word *anonymous*," Miss Brennan explained. "It means we don't know who wrote the poem. It is not the name of the poet."

More kids giggled. Millie felt sure now that she would never volunteer.

"Oh," said Howard. He began to read:

If all the world were paper
    And all the sea were ink
And all the trees were bread and cheese
    What should we do for drink? . . .

"That was a nice poem," said Miss Brennan. "You may sit down, Mr. Hall."

"Can I read mine now?" Rochelle Liederman asked, waving her hand in the air.

"Yes, you may," said Miss Brennan. Rochelle came up and found her poem. She began reading "Trees," by Joyce Kilmer:

I think that I shall never see
A poem lovely as a tree,

A tree whose hungry mouth is prest
Against the earth's sweet flowing breast—

The boys started laughing and whistling. Rochelle turned red and continued:

> A tree that looks at God all day,
> And lifts her leafy arms to pray;
>
> A tree that may in Summer wear
> A nest of robins in her hair;
>
> Upon whose bosom snow has lain—

More hoots and whistles at the word *bosom.* Millie was glad there weren't any *breasts* or *bosoms* in her poem; in case she decided to volunteer—which she didn't.

Rochelle gave Miss Brennan a look that seemed to ask if she could please sit down. Miss Brennan narrowed her eyes at the boys and motioned for her to continue. In a quavering voice, Rochelle went on:

> . . . snow has lain,
> Who intimately lives with rain;
>
> Poems are made by fools like me
> But only God can make a tree.

Rochelle hurried to her seat before the last word was even out of her mouth. Millie was sure that Rochelle wished she had chosen a different poem. But Millie liked it. She liked that it had so much to do with nature. Trees that live in snow and rain and wear robins in their hair.

"Can I read my poem?" Marlene Kaufman asked when Rochelle sat down.

"I think we've had quite enough poetry for today," said Miss Brennan, dabbing her forehead with the handkerchief she kept tucked in her sleeve. "Let's do some silent reading."

When school was over, Millie thought she would make a second attempt at selling subscriptions. She was not looking forward to it. She wasn't eager to face another person like Mr. Fink, who would blame her for the world's problems. But she knew she had to try again.

On the other hand, a new snow had begun to fall. It was fresh and clean, and Millie wanted to get to it before someone else messed it all up. And besides, she would have a chance to get some good use out of her new shovel. She could sell subscriptions another time.

Millie changed from her slacks to her leggings and put on her galoshes. Then she took her shovel from its place in the kitchen and went out. The air was clear and cold, and Millie blew out puffs of "smoke," trying to make smoke rings the way the men in the cigarette ads did.

Snow covered the ground like a clean, Rinso-white blanket, and Millie carefully stepped on the sidewalk, making clear, fresh footprints in places where no one had stepped before. With her shovel she lifted up the footprints and dumped them into a pile on the ground. Then she shoveled a path from the curb, where her father parked the car, to the entrance of her building, added that snow to her pile, and jumped into it.

She sat in the snow and pretended she was sitting in an igloo with her children, eating blubber and waiting for her Eskimo husband to come home with fish for supper. Millie had read about Alaska and Eskimos in her *Weekly Reader.* She read that it was actually very warm and cozy inside their igloos. Miss Brennan once told the class that Hawaii sounded very exotic. Millie thought that Alaska must be exotic, too. Cold, but exotic.

The sky was beginning to darken and Millie felt herself shiver. Her igloo was not warm and cozy. She knew she should not be sitting there. She should be out selling subscriptions, so she could get a bike that her mother and father would not have to pay for. She had to give the subscription-selling another chance.

Millie climbed out of her igloo, picked up her shovel, and went inside to change into some dry slacks. She gathered up her subscription forms and went back out. This time she would try the apartments at the other end of her building. There were six more apartments that were just like the ones at her end.

Millie opened the door and stepped into the dimly lit hallway. This hallway was just like hers. If somebody led her here blindfolded, and then took the blindfold off, she wouldn't be able to tell if she was in this hallway or in her own. There were the same six mailboxes to the left, and the same small eight-sided tiles on the floor and on the steps that led up to the first floor where the apartments began. Even the smell was the same at this time of the day—sort of a mingling aroma of all the suppers cooking.

Millie didn't know the people at this end of the building well at all. Maybe that was good. If they got angry at her for knocking on their doors, she didn't ever have to meet up with them again. First she would try the apartment on the left. The one where two old people lived, and where Mrs. Golub would be living if this were her side of the building.

Millie was all ready to knock when she saw a small sign on the door: SALESMEN BEWARE!

Beware? Salesmen? But Millie wasn't a salesman. Or was she? After all, she *was* selling subscriptions. And *Beware.* She didn't like that word. What should she beware of? Millie didn't need to ask for trouble. She turned and walked across to the apartment that looked like it could be hers, but belonged to a family with two small boys. She started to knock.

"Stop that!" somebody yelled. "You do that one more time and I'll break your neck!"

Quickly Millie drew her hand back. Then she heard crying coming from the other side of the door, and more yelling. "One more time! You do that one more time and you'll go to bed without supper."

It was the mother yelling at one of her sons. Millie was relieved that no one was yelling at her. But she began to worry. If this mother would break her own child's neck and send him to bed hungry, just think of what she'd do to Millie. So far, she did not like the people who lived in this part of the building.

Millie started up towards the second floor. Something was wrong. It was dark here. The light bulb must be out, Millie thought. She heard squeaking sounds on the stairs above her. The sounds seemed to be coming closer. Some of Mr. Fink's words came back to her: ". . . bad news . . . kidnappings . . ." Millie didn't need this. She didn't need any of it. She was not going to risk her life for the *Chicago Daily News.* She would just have to win her bike. She stuffed the subscription blanks in her coat pocket and ran all the way home.

Wind Poems, Sea Poems

March came with the wind blowing off Lake Michigan. And so, too, came poems of the wind. And of the sea.

Millie looked out the window at the bare tree branches bending in gusts of wind, as Angela Moretti, who was back at school, stood in front of the class reading a poem by Christina Rossetti:

Who has seen the wind?
    Neither I nor you;
But when the leaves hang trembling,
    The wind is passing through.

Who has seen the wind?
    Neither you nor I:
But when the trees bow down their heads,
    The wind is passing by.

And as she read, the trees outside the windows of Room 210 seemed to be playing a part, acting out Angela's words. The poem filled Millie with all kinds of new thoughts. You think you see the wind. But you never do. You see only what the wind does. Like when the wind blows the leaves in the fall—you see the leaves skipping along the ground. But you never really see the wind.

And she loved the line about the trees bowing down their heads. Just like the poem "Trees," which Rochelle had read, it made them seem like real people, with feelings.. Millie thought the poem was lovely.

So did Miss Brennan. "A lovely poem," she said. "But I do wish you—all of you—would try to enunciate each syllable."

If Millie were going to read her poem out loud, she would have to remember to enunciate— once she found out what the word meant.

Freddie Simon was up next. "My father was in the navy," he informed the class. "So I picked 'Sea Fever,' by John Masefield." He cleared his throat and began:

> I must go down to the seas again,
>> to the lonely sea and the sky,
> And all I ask is a tall ship
>> and a star to steer her by,

And the wheel's kick and the wind's song
   and the white sail's shaking,
And a grey mist on the sea's face
   and a grey dawn breaking . . .

"Another lovely poem," said Miss Brennan. "But it's not enough to read words. We must try to read with feeling." And she recited the first few lines of the poem in her actress voice to show what she meant by reading with feeling.

Millie thought that "Sea Fever" was beautiful, no matter how Freddie Simon had read it. She loved the mood of the poem. There was a loneliness about it, yet at the same time it made her feel safe, because of the star. And in this poem she liked the line about the sea's face. The sea had a face, just like the trees had heads and mouths and arms. She liked the way the poets made the trees and the sea seem human. Poetry, Millie noted, did not need lots of words to say a lot.

Everyone, it seemed, wanted to read. Marlene Kaufman read "Fog" by Carl Sandburg, and Millie thought it was such a sweet poem. Fog is like a cat that comes to the city on cat feet. It sits there silently, and then leaves. Miss Brennan loved that it was written by Carl Sandburg.

"I want you all to know that Carl Sandburg

is one of Chicago's very own poets. And he's one of the greatest alive today."

Alive? There were poets who were still alive? And from Chicago? This was a surprise to Millie. She would have to remember to look him up.

Now, though, Millie wanted to read her Stevenson poem. She wished that she could be as courageous as the rest of the class. But more than that, she wanted to share her "Lamplighter" with the others. She wanted them to get to know Leerie, who, like the star at sea, made her feel safe at night.

Even Sandy showed courage. She stood in front of the class and announced, " 'My Shadow,' by Robert Louis Stevenson."

"Ah, Stevenson," said Miss Brennan. "One of my favorite writers."

Millie sank down in her seat. She should have been the first one to read a Stevenson poem. Robert Louis Stevenson was her idea.

"I used to love reading *A Child's Garden of Verses* when I was a girl," Miss Brennan added.

The words took Millie by surprise. Miss Brennan was once a girl! That had to be true, of course, but it was hard to believe.

When Sandy read the poem, Millie said it with her silently, and tried to imagine herself reading the poem out loud in front of the class.

I have a little shadow
    that goes in and out with me,
And what can be the use of him
    is more than I can see.
He is very, very like me
    from the heels up to the head,
And I see him jump before me,
    when I jump into my bed.

The funniest thing about him
    is the way he likes to grow—
Not at all like proper children,
    which is always very slow;
For he sometimes shoots up taller
    like an india-rubber ball,
And he sometimes gets so little
    that there's none of him at all.

He hasn't got a notion
    of how children ought to play,
And can only make a fool of me
    in every sort of way.
He stays so close beside me,
    he's a coward you can see;
I'd think shame to stick to nursie
    as that shadow sticks to me!

One morning, very early,
    before the sun was up,

I rose and found the shining dew
    on every buttercup;
But my lazy little shadow,
    like an arrant sleepy-head,
Had stayed at home behind me
    and was fast asleep in bed.

Millie felt that she, too, was like an india-rubber ball. Bouncing up, wanting to read, and then changing her mind and bouncing back down.

Throughout the week, Millie practiced her poem at home. She practiced reading with feeling and enunciating—which meant to pronounce clearly and distinctly. She practiced reading and enunciating "It's time to take the window," so it wouldn't come out sounding like "Itstimetotake the window." Every day in school she became determined to raise her hand to volunteer. But she could never quite raise her hand high enough for Miss Brennan to see it. If everyone else could read their poems in front of a teacher who criticized, and in front of kids who laughed at each other, why couldn't she?

And every day, too, Millie checked the mail for the notice that she had won the Name Your Bicycle contest. She listened to the radio and heard the announcer promise that the winners' names would be picked very soon.

For Millie, it would never be soon enough.

Last Chance

What was so great about *Torpedo*? Or *Jupiter*? It was Thursday, and Millie had just heard the names of the winners over the radio. Some boy in Muncie, Indiana, had named his bicycle *Torpedo*. And a girl from Kalamazoo, Michigan, had called hers *Jupiter*. Millie couldn't believe it. Her names were just as good. Better, even. Why hadn't she won?

Millie turned off the radio and moped into the kitchen. "They could have at least picked someone from Chicago," she told her mother. "I never even heard of Muncie or Kalamazoo." She sat down on her window seat and sighed deeply. "I'll probably never get my bike now. I'll probably get it when I'm in high school. And then I'll be too old to ride it." In the back of her mind were nagging thoughts reminding her that she could still sell subscriptions, but she pushed them away.

"Nothing comes before its time," said Mrs. Cooper, who was unpacking grocery bags.

"Well, speaking of time," said Millie, "tomorrow is the last time we get to read our poems. Our last chance. Miss Brennan said so today."

Millie's mother washed two apples and gave one to Millie. "Haven't you read yours yet?"

"No," said Millie, taking a bite of the apple. "And I don't know if I'm going to. I want to, but I don't want to. There must be something wrong with me. I'm afraid to stand up and read in front of everybody, and in front of Miss Brennan. She almost never has anything nice to say. I'm one of the only ones who hasn't read yet. Me and Ronald Van Buskirk." Ronald Van Buskirk was the only boy in Millie's class who had yellow hair.

"Did you know," said Millie's mother, sitting down next to Millie on the window seat, "that Alfred, Lord Tennyson, once won a prize for a poem he wrote called 'Timbuctoo,' but he was too shy to read it at the award ceremony?"

Millie stopped chewing and looked up at her mother. "Really? Tennyson? The one who wrote about the Light Brigade?"

Her mother nodded.

"Wow," said Millie. If a famous poet like Tennyson could be shy, there was nothing wrong with Millie if she was shy. Even so, she should bounce up like that india-rubber ball and read her poem.

"Why don't you try to pretend you're reading the poem in your own room and you're reading to yourself? Or to us?" her mother offered. "It might make it easier for you."

The next morning Miss Brennan made an announcement. "Today will be the last day for our poetry readings. So if you plan to read, this is your last chance. Who has not read yet, but wants to?"

Millie tried to raise her hand, but she couldn't lift it off her lap. Some india-rubber ball *she* was.

Ronald Van Buskirk raised his hand and Miss Brennan called on him.

"I wanted to do something by Longfellow," said Ronald. "Like 'The Wreck of the Hesperus' or 'Paul Revere's Ride.' But the poems were too long."

"Longfellow writes long poems," Howard Hall called out. "Longfellow, long poems, get it?"

Miss Brennan shut him up with one of her cold stares and told Ronald Van Buskirk to continue.

"So I picked 'Hide and Seek' by Robin Christopher." Ronald went on to read something about a kid who hides and tries to find himself:

> . . . I hide myself
> Behind myself
> And then I try
> To find myself . . .

"He should get lost and stay lost," said Howard Hall to O.C. Goodwin, in a voice loud enough for the rest of the class to hear. Millie wished Howard Hall would be the one to get lost.

She hardly paid any attention to the rest of the poem. Or to Ronald Van Buskirk's yellow hair. She was too busy worrying about her own poem. She was trembling, the way she did when she had a fever.

After Ronald was finished, a girl came up and read something about wanting to be a lighthouse.

"You look like a lighthouse," O.C. Goodwin called out.

Millie wished that O.C. Goodwin and Howard Hall would disappear for the day. They were always making wisecracks, but today of all days, they were making more than usual.

"Anyone else?" Miss Brennan interrupted Millie's thoughts. "Is there anyone who wants to read?" She looked around the room. "Remember, class, this is your last chance."

Chance. Millie had to take it. Her hand shot up in the air.

"Very well, Miss Cooper. Please come up."

Millie walked over to the wooden box and found her poem among the few papers left. Then she turned to face the class. "The Lamplighter," she began, "by Robert Louis Stevenson." That's as far as she got. Suddenly the words jumped out at her. And then they began to blur. She couldn't read her own handwriting. She wished she had written more neatly. But then a thought came to her. She didn't have to read. She had the words written in her memory.

Millie looked across the classroom at the blackboard, and her mother's voice came back to her. "Just pretend you're in your own room, and you're reciting to yourself."

So Millie began to recite "The Lamplighter." And as she recited, she imagined Leerie in the black top hat and long, black coat that he wore in the picture in her book. And she pretended she was in her own room at home, reciting her favorite poem as she had done so many times before.

My tea is nearly ready
    and the sun has left the sky,
It's time to take the window
    to see Leerie going by;
For every night at tea-time
    and before you take your seat,
With lantern and with ladder
    he comes posting up the street.

Now Tom would be a driver
and Maria go to sea,
And my papa's a banker
and as rich as he can be;
But I, when I am stronger
and can choose what I'm to do,
O Leerie, I'll go round at night
and light the lamps with you!

For we are very lucky
with a lamp before the door,
And Leerie stops to light it
as he lights so many more;
And O! before you hurry by
with ladder and with light,
O Leerie, see a little child
and nod to him tonight!

The class was silent when Millie came back from her imaginary trip with Leerie. Nobody said a word. Not her classmates, not Miss Brennan. She didn't know what to do. Should she keep standing there or go back to her seat?

Finally, Miss Brennan stood up and walked over to her. "Miss Cooper," she began, and Millie's heart sank. What had she done wrong? Maybe she had mumbled. Or read without feeling. "Miss Cooper, I must say that in all my years of teaching, I have rarely heard such a

beautiful poetry recitation from one of my pupils."

Millie blinked. She wanted to make sure she really was back in Room 210.

"You recited with so much feeling and expression I could tell that you loved the poem. Robert Louis Stevenson would be proud of you."

Millie was overcome with joy. She couldn't wait to get home to tell her mother that she had had the most wonderful day! And all because she had taken a chance. She told her father, too, the second he walked in the door. She didn't even wait for him to take off his hat and coat.

She told them again at supper. "And nobody laughed at me, and I was the only one who knew their poem by heart, and Miss Brennan said that Robert Louis Stevenson would be proud of me."

"He couldn't be prouder than we are," said her father.

Her mother nodded. "We're proud that you did such a good job with the poem and proud that you took the chance." She smiled at Millie and nodded again. "It looks like our little girl is growing up."

Blue, and
Fully Equipped

It stood in the middle of the kitchen floor, gleaming in the morning sunlight. Millie rubbed her eyes to make sure she was really awake. That she wasn't dreaming. But this wasn't a dream. It was still there. The most beautiful blue girl's bicycle! Fully equipped with balloon tires, a tank, and a luggage carrier.

She reached out to it and the next thing she knew she was straddling the bicycle and holding on to the handlebars. She ran her hands over the shiny metal frame and touched everything: the seat, the pedals, the spokes.

"Does it meet with your approval?"

Millie's father was standing in the doorway. Her mother was next to him. Millie ran to them and hugged them both. "Oh, it's the best bicycle in the world," she said, jumping up and down. "Thank you, thank you, thank you."

Then she stopped jumping. "But my birthday isn't until June."

"Well," her mother said, "we didn't want you to miss all those good riding days in March, April, and May."

Millie ran back to the bike. "I can't wait. I'm going to ride it this very second."

"Hold your horses," said her mother. "You're still in your pajamas."

"And I want to go out with you the first time," her father told her. "You haven't had much experience, you know."

"And then can I go riding with Sandy?" Millie asked.

"Maybe. First let's see how you do right around here." The three of them sat down at the kitchen table and admired the bicycle.

"Beautiful," said Millie.

"Very streamlined," said her mother.

"Fully equipped," said her father. "Can I borrow it some time so I can bicycle my way to a healthy tan?"

"How about me?" her mother asked. "Then I can shed my girdle and keep my girlish figure." She struck a pinup-girl pose.

"You can both ride it whenever you want to," Millie said, laughing. And then she asked, "What made you decide to buy it for me?"

"Well," said her father, "we decided that if you could take a chance with your poem and your subscriptions, then we could take a chance too. Just like we had to take a chance the first time we let you cross the street by yourself. Or let you go to school alone."

"Does that mean you won't worry about me when I ride my bike?" Millie asked.

"Oh, we'll worry all right," her mother said. "Especially me. In the beginning, at least. Every time you go out on that bike I'll worry. But I know I have to let you do it. And I know that you'll be responsible."

"Oh, I will," Millie assured her mother. "I promise."

Millie looked around the kitchen, at her new bicycle, and at the snow shovel standing against the door. Later she would put the shovel in the basement shed and keep it there until next winter.

But now it was the first week of spring, bicycle riding time. Millie went to her room to change into a sweater and blue jeans. She rolled up the right cuff of her jeans so it wouldn't get caught in the bicycle chain.

Her earmuffs, unworn since February, lay on top of the dresser next to *A Child's Garden of Verses* and her valentine from Sandy. Next year she would take a chance with her valentines. Maybe she would get lots of them and maybe she would get just a few. But she would take the chance.

Millie picked up her earmuffs and kissed the tips of Mickey's noses. Then she tucked them away in the bottom drawer of her dresser.

"Good-bye, Mickey Mouse," she whispered. "See you next winter."